Thieves & Kings

Thieves & Kings Volume Five, copyright ©2004 Mark Oakley. All rights reserved. No part of this book may be reproduced in any manner whatsoever without prior written permission except in the context of reviews. For information contact *I Box Publishing*, P.O. Box 2414, Wolfville, Nova Scotia B4P 2S3 Canada or e-mail through the company website at: ***www.iboxpublishing.com***

ISBN: 0-9681025-4-9

Printed in Canada

I Box Publishing welcomes any comments or questions at the above address, and may publish/answer them in the letters pages of the on-going comic book series, available at finer comic shops everywhere.

Thieves & Kings is a long story which spans several books. At the time of this printing, five of those books had been produced, and a number of original comics were still available. If you are interested in purchasing copies directly from *I Box Publishing*, your order would be happily filled. Send a letter asking for ordering information or check out the company website for the most current pricing. (Both address are listed above.)

As it turns out. . ,
Stories are *not* just air and ink.
Who would have thought?
The act of imagining gives life.
Not some poetic metaphor,
But *Life!*
—In other worlds not so distant,
I am imagining you right now,
And you are never, never, never, alone.

Chapter 1

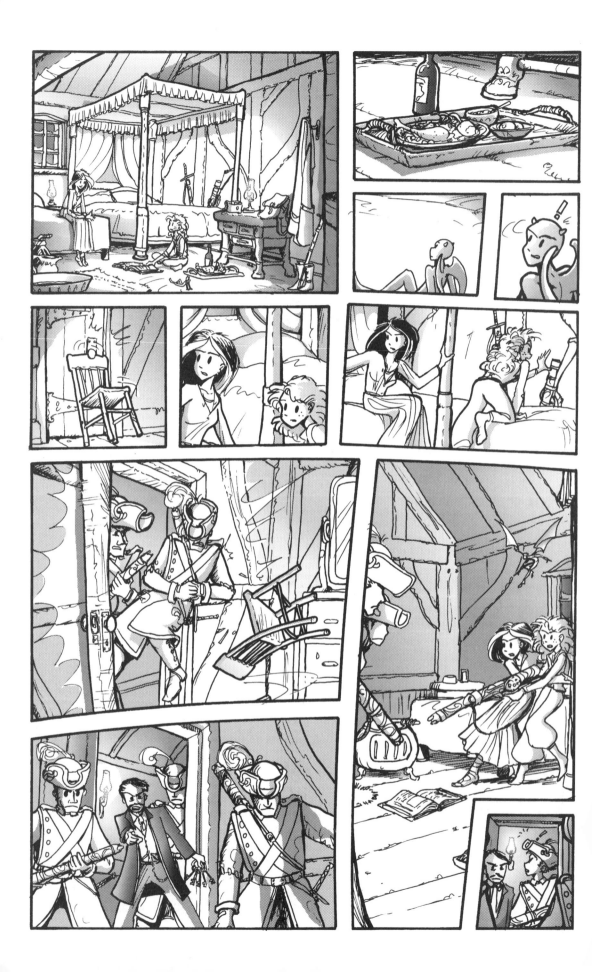

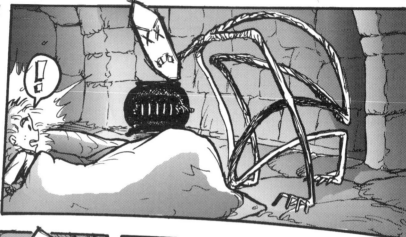

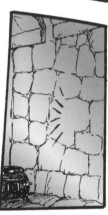

And so the weeks went by.

The Winter months proved to be some of the best of their lives. —And well deserved! Each of them, Rubel, Heath and the new one, with her rosy cheeks and black hair, had spent the summer working through hard and harrowing trials of life, made from painful choices and difficult fights of both body and heart. It had been a long Summer indeed!

Yet, because each had survived without getting too badly hurt, and because young people do not think of time quite the same way older ones do, those trials were in the distant past. Their lives were now lit with the glow of fun and love and easy living; which was, for the two girls especially, a welcome change. Having a thief like Rubel for a friend meant wanting for very little.

Heath set the rules.

No poor people, (they had enough troubles). No merchants. —Except the mean ones and the crafty ones. And no rich people who were good at heart. Because that would be Wrong.

Rubel, of course, had already worked these matters out when he was small, but Heath was firm nonetheless. It still left a lot of places from which to steal the things they needed. Rather *too* many places, Heath reflected somberly.

The stones were a problem, however. Who would have thought? Where does one find good stones in a city? Try it sometime! They're atrociously heavy; you can only really carry one or two at a time, and most of the good ones are already being used for something which would be disastrous to take apart. Of course, you could always pay somebody to cut new stones from a quarry and cart them to you. Heath wasn't stupid, after all. But still. . . "They're *rocks!*" She threw up her hands in a comedic appeal to the heavens. "The whole world is *made* out of rocks! You shouldn't have to *pay* for rocks, for goodness sake!" Kim, Rubel and Varkias all laughed at the obvious sense of this, putting an immediate end to the idea. Of course, it still left her with the problem. . . But she was working on it.

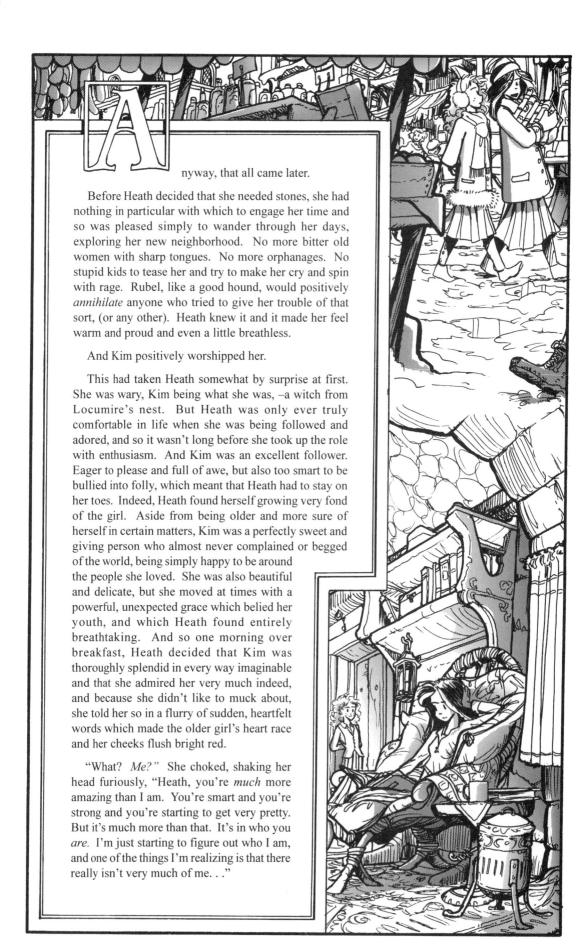

Anyway, that all came later.

Before Heath decided that she needed stones, she had nothing in particular with which to engage her time and so was pleased simply to wander through her days, exploring her new neighborhood. No more bitter old women with sharp tongues. No more orphanages. No stupid kids to tease her and try to make her cry and spin with rage. Rubel, like a good hound, would positively *annihilate* anyone who tried to give her trouble of that sort, (or any other). Heath knew it and it made her feel warm and proud and even a little breathless.

And Kim positively worshipped her.

This had taken Heath somewhat by surprise at first. She was wary, Kim being what she was, –a witch from Locumire's nest. But Heath was only ever truly comfortable in life when she was being followed and adored, and so it wasn't long before she took up the role with enthusiasm. And Kim was an excellent follower. Eager to please and full of awe, but also too smart to be bullied into folly, which meant that Heath had to stay on her toes. Indeed, Heath found herself growing very fond of the girl. Aside from being older and more sure of herself in certain matters, Kim was a perfectly sweet and giving person who almost never complained or begged of the world, being simply happy to be around the people she loved. She was also beautiful and delicate, but she moved at times with a powerful, unexpected grace which belied her youth, and which Heath found entirely breathtaking. And so one morning over breakfast, Heath decided that Kim was thoroughly splendid in every way imaginable and that she admired her very much indeed, and because she didn't like to muck about, she told her so in a flurry of sudden, heartfelt words which made the older girl's heart race and her cheeks flush bright red.

"What? *Me?*" She choked, shaking her head furiously, "Heath, you're *much* more amazing than I am. You're smart and you're strong and you're starting to get very pretty. But it's much more than that. It's in who you *are*. I'm just starting to figure out who I am, and one of the things I'm realizing is that there really isn't very much of me..."

S he gazed sadly off into space for a moment as she considered her own words. "You always seem to be so *passionate* about things. I don't understand how you do that."

She paused for a long moment, seeming to struggle with something in her mind, debating whether or not she should say more. At that moment Rubel bounded in amidst a swirl of snow particles turned golden in the morning sun, a boyish grin on his face, a bulging sack over one shoulder and Varkias dancing on his other, both adventurers filled with laughter and stories to tell. Kim let out her breath and didn't finish what she was thinking. The two girls basked in his light, and he in theirs, for while fairy tale magic hummed in his blood, the girls both had sorcerer magic coursing in theirs. Together, the three of them were mythical. They were even partly aware of this in a self-conscious kind of way, but not nearly so much as it was actually true. Only Varkias understood just how far it went, but he wasn't the sort to waste time contemplating such things. And so, the small band warmed their home and ate and played through their winter days, filling their world with a light which the shopkeepers and market people could almost feel.

As such, it wasn't long at all before the world around began showing signs of being affected by their presence. Wider smiles, warmer greetings and brisker sales. Though, it wasn't until Heath finally made up her mind that, like a bright puzzle piece locking into place, things changed utterly and for good.

It went like this...

Kim was sitting naked in a wooden tub, its sides sloshing over with hot and soapy bath water, while Rubel scrubbed her back and kissed her skin. He padded about her like a tiger with sparking, lusty eyes so that she thrilled and cooed the way lovers do. Heath, feeling in the way, escaped to the roof.

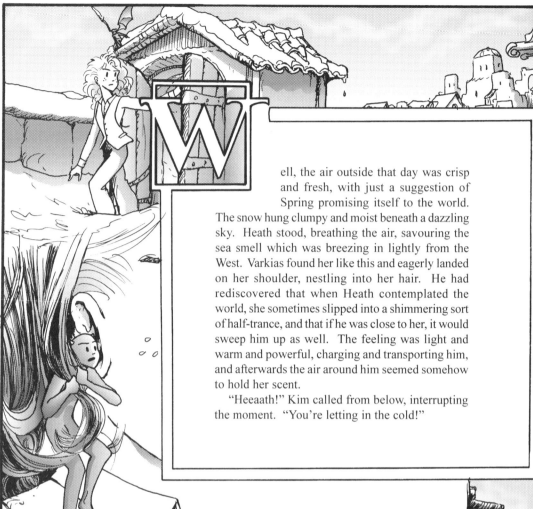

Well, the air outside that day was crisp and fresh, with just a suggestion of Spring promising itself to the world. The snow hung clumpy and moist beneath a dazzling sky. Heath stood, breathing the air, savouring the sea smell which was breezing in lightly from the West. Varkias found her like this and eagerly landed on her shoulder, nestling into her hair. He had rediscovered that when Heath contemplated the world, she sometimes slipped into a shimmering sort of half-trance, and that if he was close to her, it would sweep him up as well. The feeling was light and warm and powerful, charging and transporting him, and afterwards the air around him seemed somehow to hold her scent.

"Heeaath!" Kim called from below, interrupting the moment. "You're letting in the cold!"

Varkias grumbled aloud, "Idiots. I liked it a lot better before they met! They should know that you live here, too!"

Heath was unconcerned, her thoughts far away. She climbed the rest of the way out and shut the door behind her. Then, picking her way through the snow, she climbed the riser to a patch on the curving rooftop which had melted clear and was drying in the sun, almost threatening to be warm. She sat there and gazed again over the market below.

"You'll freeze," Varkias complained, releasing himself from her sandy curls. "You should get your coat."

"Ahh..," Heath breathed, as the odd thoughts which had been stirring for weeks now, began tugging again at her mind, picking up speed, taking shape. The colorful market spread out like a large, complicated toy below. A glow began to spread over her face.

"What?" The imp peered at her. "The market?"

She grinned and then laughed aloud. "It's so beautiful!" Standing, she walked along the rooftop ridge, surveying the scene below her. Varkias felt an involuntary shiver travel up his spine. Without looking, she hopped to the next tier and stood, hands on her hips, surveying, face beaming. She gazed for a long moment and then looked across at one of the crumbled walls which leaned against the southern end of their home. She went to it and kicked some snow from its stony forehead. It almost looked like a flight of stairs. "Oh, Varkias!" she gushed, turning to the imp. "I know what we have to *do!* I *know* why we're *here!"*

Varkias followed in a fluster. "You'll get frostbite." –But his heart was soaring up and away with hers.

With footsteps full of purpose, she descended the crumbling wall without using her hands, knocking down clumps of snow and rotted brick as she went. She hopped the last little way to the street, landing with a scrunch in a damp snowbank. "These can be the stairs!" she announced proudly to herself and to the world.

"Stairs?"

"Yes. There's a lot we have to do! A lot we have to find!" she enthused. "We'll need a sign, and ropes and lanterns and something for a roof. And I *must* learn all my spells!" She counted the items out loud, her mind racing as she set off into the wilds of the market with the imp close behind. She paused briefly to look back at the crumbling wall. "And I think we'll have to find some new stones."

The two sorceresses crouched together in secret council, neither appearing to notice the winter chill. Their eyes burned with power as they spoke.

"She is being careless," said one. "She is too young to make her stand. It is too soon."

"Time has run out," the other replied. "Another year would prove disastrous. Her choice is made."

"Hm. Her dreaming awake is without discipline. She pulls her party into danger; their minds are already caught up. She has made them forget that they are hunted! She dreams of warmth and of games. A fool's dream. A *child's* dream!"

"Her thief knows the danger. Her mists cannot envelope him. The wizard made him so."

"He may not be able to scoop her to safety this time. Locumire has her pieces in place. I can feel her eagerness on the wind! And the prince will no longer be put off."

"This is true... Yes. They will live or they will die and it will happen very soon. The thief knows that this battle is not a joke, but he also trusts in her intuition, and so should we. The Red Sorceress is our teacher, and when she left her last instructions, they were very clear."

"Hm . . . I wonder if this lesson will prove to be our last."

Catastrophe's eyes, smoldering grey, gazed in thought.

"All the more reason to learn it well."

Chapter 2

HEATH!

WHERE DID YOU GO? -YOU JUST VANISHED!

I WAS GETTING SOME OF THE THINGS WE'LL NEED.

I FIGURED IT ALL OUT!

FIGURED WHAT OUT?

DID YOU BUY ALL THAT STUFF?

IT'S ON CREDIT.

CREDIT?

IS THAT A NEW COAT?

"He made the tower for a reason," she explained. "It wasn't just to live in. It was there to provide a *middle*. A place that all his friends would think about when they thought of him and of all the important things he was doing. It took all of those ideas and focused them and made them real. The Monster Slayers *came* from that tower. They came from *Quinton*, and we were both part of it, each in our own times. The Monster Slayers are a *very* powerful idea."

"How?" Kim asked intently, "Explain it to me again." She looked back and forth between the two. Rubel and Heath had both tried to describe that strange children's secret society to her before, only to discover that it was a surprisingly difficult concept to couch in words. Kim remained fascinated and mystified. "It was *real* monsters sometimes, wasn't it?"

"You bet! Heath captured Jurid and put him in a bottle!" Varkias said proudly, as though he had been there himself. "And me and Rubel and our gang fought *Chead* once, and we won!"

"But I still don't get it," Kim pressed, turning to Rubel. "You were just kids, and you describe it as fighting pretend monsters, but then later you talk about the same ones as if they were real. You switch around! It's really confusing! Were there *really* monsters living under your friend's bed?"

"Actually. . ," Rubel thought, "it's sometimes hard to remember. I didn't even remember Chead until recently."

"But that's just it," Heath urged, her expression burning. *"None* of it was pretend. That's the whole point. It's about *perceptions*. There's *real* power in this! It's easier for kids, and that's why Quinton always starts training us when we're so young. Our job is to not let that power drain away as we grow up.

"Except," Rubel frowned. "Some of it *was* pretend."

"No!" Heath shook her head. "You're not getting it. It's about *perceptions,"* she repeated, using the word she had picked up from her magic book. "All the things we see and do here are just *metaphors.* Those monsters that you were sure were real and that you really did fight, they were just times when the metaphor gained *power.* –When your strength of mind was enough to see what was actually there. Get it?"

"Ahhh. . ," Rubel nodded, a spark of partial understanding flickering in his mind. Beside him, Kim nodded similarly, though the only thing either of them fully grasped was that Heath clearly saw something entirely dazzling which they did not. Heath blazed back at them, one side of her face flushed pink from the heat of the brass furnace, giving her a slightly feverish expression. She held them with her eyes, enthusiastic, intense, watching them for signs of understanding. They tried, but could only watch her back with tingling spines. After a moment, she released them and shook her head. She took a sip from her hot chocolate, wiped her mouth on the back of her hand, and looked up again at them both with fondness and forgiveness.

"Well anyway," she went on, "that's what Quinton was doing. He was preparing us. He was forging a pathway in our minds so we could *see.* And that's what we're going to do here!"

"Hmph. Well, *I* understand," Varkias said stolidly. They all looked at him. "She wants us to build a new base for the Monster Slayers. How confusing is that?"

"I wish I'd been with you," Kim sighed winsomely. "I hope I meet Quinton someday."

"You had your own preparation," Heath assured. "You can see magic just fine. In fact, I think we need you especially. You can see *black* magic."

"So what exactly do you want me to build, then?" Rubel asked. "Before, we were just talking about an extra room up on the roof for you to sleep in."

"Well, we still need that," Heath growled. "This place wasn't built for three people at all." Rubel and Kim shuffled uncomfortably and avoided Heath's gaze. "But more important," she added. "It'll be our shop front. Where Kim and I will work. The stairs going up and the sign have to be ready for spring. And I think a canopy or something for shade. And some tall plants. It has to look really nice, and it has to be warm feeling. It has to be something people will look up and see and feel really good about, but also a little mystified. Their hearts have to swell!"

"Hmm." Rubel looked thoughtful. "Well, I'm not a master architect. . . I can build something that works, and I can try to make it look nice, but I don't know if I can make people's hearts *swell*. It's just stones and woodwork, after all. . ."

"Don't worry," Heath assured. "You'll make it just right. I've watched the way you are when you build things around here. In fact, I think you're the *only* one who can do it just right. Trust me. It'll take care of itself. It's *trying* to be. I can *feel* it for sure, now. All we have to do is help it along." She sat up and leaned in with her pink cheeks and fiery eyes, and she held them in her gaze for another moment during which Rubel and Kim did not breathe. "Locumire is working to make the rest of the city feel mean and dangerous and dark," she told them. *"This* part of the city is going to be *ours."*

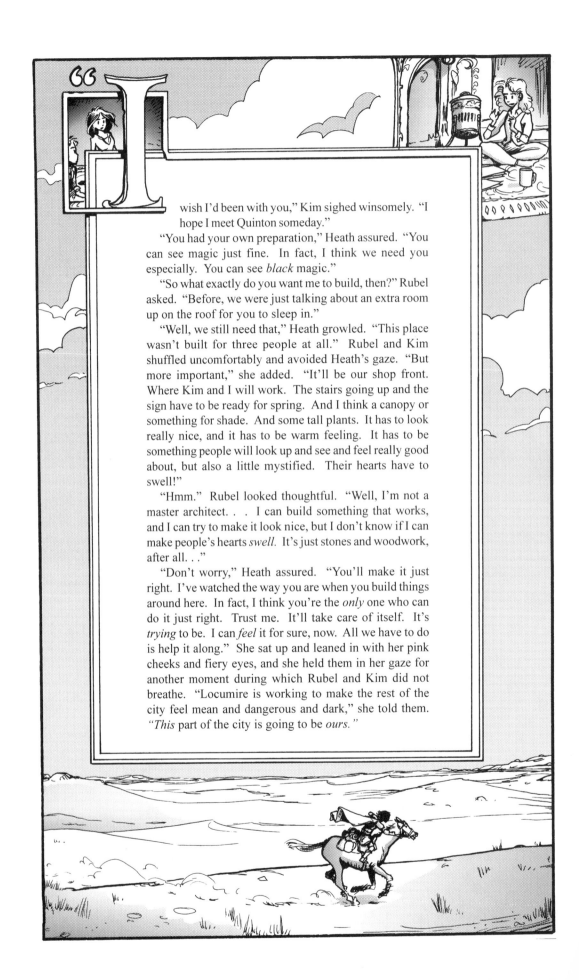

Chapter 3

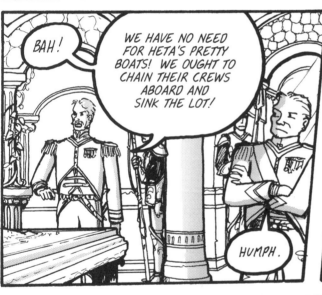

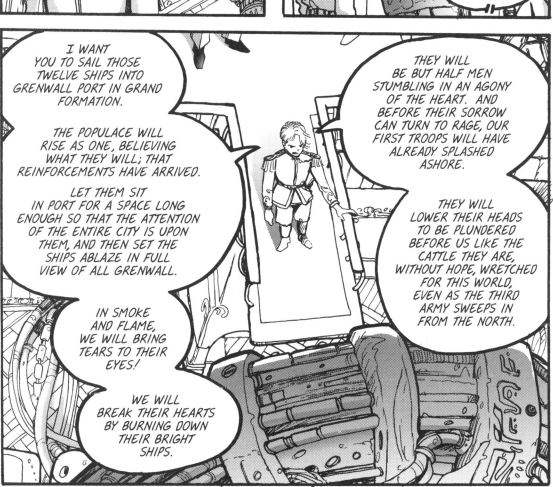

Chapter 4

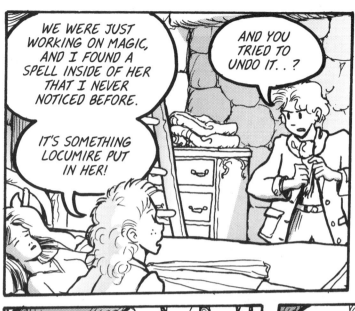

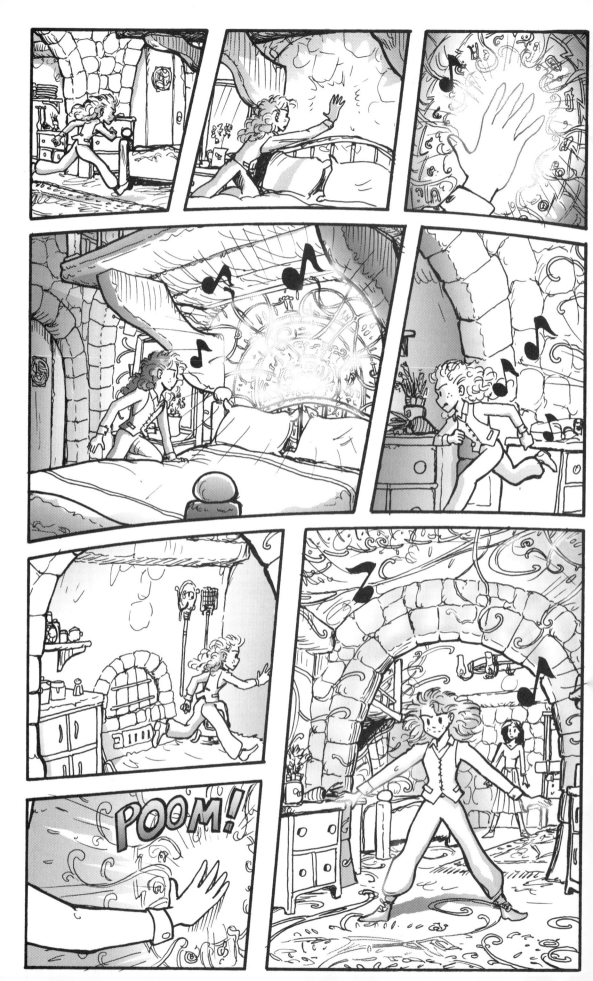

Rubel reacted in a blur, dodging the grasp of the frightful creature, flicking the stained glass mer-sword at her so that it tugged lightly in his hand as it caught flesh and drew blood. The apparition shrieked in surprise and pain, flying back from the door with smoke trailing from its wound. The glass blade, swirling with emerald and ruby light, had been a special gift from both Soracia and his two mermaid friends. Soracia had instructed carefully where the pair ought to search, half-way across the sea and beneath a sunken palace from an age lost in time. The two mermaids bit their lips prettily and Soracia laughed at them with gusto, though in truth, even she was anxious about his welfare. "You have to be careful, Rubel," they told him. "Witches are stronger than you. Thieves are awful with magic! It's your soft spot, and they know it."

"That sword was made to cut through just the kind of magic Locumire uses. The kind she is a slave to," Soracia explained. "But you must be careful!"

"Yes! You must," chimed the mermaids, cuddling up to the edge of the pool where he stood above them. "We didn't even know if we should give it to you at all!"

"But why not?"

"That sword was made in a special way," Soracia told him. "If you lose heart while using it. . , if you get in your own way with uncertainties or tangled thoughts, it will shatter. —And if it breaks while you are holding it, then your heart will stop beating and you will die in that very same instant. You must be *very* careful, Rubel! You must act and think in one motion. Never with self-doubt. Do you understand?"

"Ha! Of course I do," Rubel had assured them, gleaming with confidence. "I never lose heart in a fight. —Not when it's for a good reason!" The mermaids made more nervous sounds and chewed their pretty lips and tried to make him promise things he didn't listen to. Instead he swung the flashing blade and leaped like a cat about the water cave, laughing and crying things like, "Hah!" and "Ho there!" Soracia's heart beat hard and she watched him with a fond smile, but also with a hunger she did not show.

Heaving against the magical pull which had flung the door open, Rubel managed to close and bar it again, shutting out the blast of wind and snow. Heath was ready, and pressed her hand to the center of the door, triggering the ward spell she had hidden there. —From her fingers another spider's web of light leaped across the wood and stone, intricate patterns flashing alive. All the other patterns she had activated around the room then pulsed once more together as they all intertwined, forming a final, important connection.

There were always protection spells surrounding their home; every moment of every day. Heath had put them there to guard and warn and such, but *this* spell was special, the very strongest she could muster, meant for just such a time as this. And as the centerpiece of that spell was activated upon the door, Heath's fortress was complete. A feeling of vast power surged through the room; the door and walls and everything surrounding them seemed to almost clench and shift slightly, as though scrunching more firmly into place, locked and secure. The air inside grew immediately silent; the candles settled down from their excited flickering, illuminating everything around them in a steady golden glow.

The two girls, the boy and the imp all held their breaths, each feeling a little dizzied by the change. The new silence was strong and rich and somehow nourishing, causing the sense of danger outside to recede, seeming now at once both unimportant and very distant. Rubel let his breath out slowly and backed up from the door. He'd felt this kind of magic before, he thought slowly. He looked about the chamber, feeling an unconscious smile touch his face. The muscles in his neck and shoulders tingled pleasantly and he grinned openly. It was like being in the heart of the Sleeping Wood, he realized all at once.

"It's like Summer time!", Kim gasped aloud. "Oh, Heath! How *did* you?"

Rubel regarded her thoughtfully, and Heath returned his gaze with smiling, sparking eyes. She was quickly becoming skilled in her work.

"Nice job," he nodded to her. "This is good."

She beamed at him.

"Thanks! I thought you'd like it."

The reprieve only lasted a few moments. They felt the shock come through the earth and stone, causing the air to compress slightly around them as the sound penetrated. BOOM! Something very large slammed against the door. Heath's ward spell, however, repelled the aggressor with ease, making them all feel as though they had been tickled. Whatever it was on the outside was not at all pleased by this and it let out an unearthly roar into the night. The golden calm of Heath's spell was unaffected, rolling about them, making the attack seem futile and even rather silly. They all chuckled and shook their heads the same way one does when witnessing a petulant person complain and huff and make an embarrassing display over something minor.

"How long can you hold them?" Rubel asked, returning his attention to the door. He turned the glass hilt of the mer-sword in his hand.

"I don't actually know." Heath admitted, frowning slightly. "I'm still just remembering how to do this."

As if in response, the earth thumped once more, shaking this time a few siftings of dust from between the stones of the ceiling. The wood of the door creaked slightly.

"Yeah, well, whatever happens," Varkias muttered under his breath, "they're going to be in for a bigger fight than they realize!" He held the poisoned sting-needle he had fetched like a spear and leveled his narrow-eyed determination upon the door. "They have to fight *me* before I'll let them hurt any of you!"

They each felt a brief flutter of both surprise and pride at hearing Varkias speak. For some reason, it was easy to forget that he understood love.

"Just don't do anything foolish," Rubel cautioned. "Now get ready. Something is about to happen. . ."

The four held their breaths a long moment, each awaiting the next thing that would happen. Heath blew a thread of hair from her face as she strained to keep the ceiling intact. With her teeth clenched, she watched the dark gap, and for several long moments only flurries and storm winds wailed down into the crumbling chamber. And then.., a tendril of oily smoke slid over the edge of the stone. —Like smoke but *not...* It did not move in the air as smoke ought to have done. It did not blow with the wind as real smoke should. Rather it was heavy and deliberate. *Alive.*

In a fluid rope, syrup-like, the dark substance fell, half pooling, half coiling itself upon the floor. Rubel and the girls watched with awful fascination until all at once in a foul torrent, Jurid's entire form vomited down through the hole, splashing across the ground in a frightening rush. They all jumped back from the black lake edge of Jurid's mass even as the beast rose up, its cloaked form expanding all the way to the groaning ceiling. The nightmare shape heaved as though drawing a deep breath, and the room grew cold. It regarded them, holding the four of them in its gaze for a cold fraction of a moment and then, a mountain of pulsing black, Jurid plummeted down upon them.

"NOW, Heath!" Rubel cried, pulling Kim backwards with him into the kitchen alcove.

Heath let out a cry of effort even as Jurid flew at her. The monster was strong now, far more so than when Heath had last met it in the daylight of Millbrook's friendly wood. It had been groomed and fed in darkest ways in the very bowls of Locumire's nest. —Ways only such beasts as it understood and craved. Heath recoiled and clenched with her hands and with her mind, taking all the stone above, and brought it collapsing down upon the beast with all her might!

The broken lines of her protective strong-ward spell were still active, spider webbing their way in bright silver pathways through and over the stone, flashing in the darkness, netting the beast, holding it beneath the pile even as the hurricane of frozen wind and flurries exploded in the atmosphere around them.

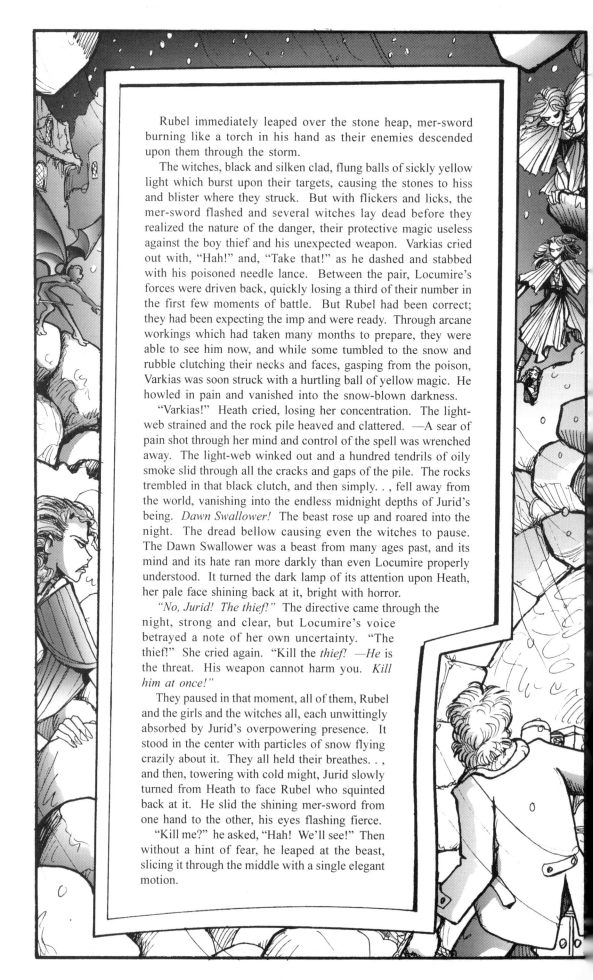

Rubel immediately leaped over the stone heap, mer-sword burning like a torch in his hand as their enemies descended upon them through the storm.

The witches, black and silken clad, flung balls of sickly yellow light which burst upon their targets, causing the stones to hiss and blister where they struck. But with flickers and licks, the mer-sword flashed and several witches lay dead before they realized the nature of the danger, their protective magic useless against the boy thief and his unexpected weapon. Varkias cried out with, "Hah!" and, "Take that!" as he dashed and stabbed with his poisoned needle lance. Between the pair, Locumire's forces were driven back, quickly losing a third of their number in the first few moments of battle. But Rubel had been correct; they had been expecting the imp and were ready. Through arcane workings which had taken many months to prepare, they were able to see him now, and while some tumbled to the snow and rubble clutching their necks and faces, gasping from the poison, Varkias was soon struck with a hurtling ball of yellow magic. He howled in pain and vanished into the snow-blown darkness.

"Varkias!" Heath cried, losing her concentration. The light-web strained and the rock pile heaved and clattered. —A sear of pain shot through her mind and control of the spell was wrenched away. The light-web winked out and a hundred tendrils of oily smoke slid through all the cracks and gaps of the pile. The rocks trembled in that black clutch, and then simply. . , fell away from the world, vanishing into the endless midnight depths of Jurid's being. *Dawn Swallower!* The beast rose up and roared into the night. The dread bellow causing even the witches to pause. The Dawn Swallower was a beast from many ages past, and its mind and its hate ran more darkly than even Locumire properly understood. It turned the dark lamp of its attention upon Heath, her pale face shining back at it, bright with horror.

"No, Jurid! The thief!" The directive came through the night, strong and clear, but Locumire's voice betrayed a note of her own uncertainty. "The thief!" She cried again. "Kill the *thief!* —He is the threat. His weapon cannot harm you. *Kill him at once!"*

They paused in that moment, all of them, Rubel and the girls and the witches all, each unwittingly absorbed by Jurid's overpowering presence. It stood in the center with particles of snow flying crazily about it. They all held their breathes. . , and then, towering with cold might, Jurid slowly turned from Heath to face Rubel who squinted back at it. He slid the shining mer-sword from one hand to the other, his eyes flashing fierce.

"Kill me?" he asked, "Hah! We'll see!" Then without a hint of fear, he leaped at the beast, slicing it through the middle with a single elegant motion.

urid shrieked and the glass shone like white metal from a smithie's forge, but the beast remained whole. It gushed after the boy like a python made from oil and silk, and the two vanished into the night as well, leaving Heath and Kim alone before the remaining witches.

"And now. . ." Locumire said, surging from the darkness, flanked by six hot-eyed and angry young women with clawed hands and crackles of power and expensive hair no longer in place. The two kitchen lamps still alight danced orange light across the woman's face as she stood like piece of the very storm itself and gazed imperiously down upon them.

"You don't scare me," Heath said, unable to think of anything better to say. —It was true at least, though she could not have explained why. Locumire snorted a laugh back at her.

"You are a very lucky child," she said. "I was weaving something which would have hurt you a great deal more than what I am forced to do now."

"Hah," Heath scoffed back. "Kim couldn't hurt me. You think your magic is so special! I'm still just re-learning how sorcery works, but I can already tell that you don't understand things at all! Kim was never going to hurt me or Rubel, no matter what you think you could have done with her! Everything is happening like this for a reason. I didn't find that spell you put in her by *luck*. You don't get it at all! Not at all!"

Locumire, her platinum hair cascading around her perfect face, frowned and took a step forward. Her hand flashed out and Heath threw up her own in defense, but the magic light in her palm only spattered like a knocked drink, vanishing in the air. Locumire laughed and snatched a handful of Heath's hair and drew the girl close.

"You don't know nearly enough to speak so boldly, child. The universe does not play favorites. It rewards only those strong enough to do as they will. You do have some power, but you are young, and without your friends I have a great deal more of it than you. You will learn that under my care, I think. You will learn *respect.*"

"Let go of me!" Heath demanded, struggling.

"Dorthmina," Locumire called out to one of her girls. "The carriage."

"Yes, my lady.'

"What should we do with Kimithin?" another asked, casting a look at Kim who stood clutching her fists in the gathering darkness, feeling angry and frightened and useless.

Locumire paused and gazed at the girl for a moment. "Leave her here on her own. Let her live in the world she has chosen. If she comes back to us, perhaps we will let her in again. Lehanna will decide."

With that, Heath was bundled off into the waiting carriage and the witches departed into the night.

Chapter 5

You see, going too far in either direction can end in a hopeless, helpless state of affairs. Being without feelings is a comfortable place to be in times of crisis; without feelings, one cannot hurt. The difficulty is that while the mind might feel safe, the body left uncared for is at the mercy of whatever dangers are present. And yet if one does allow feelings during a crisis, then there is the danger of being hurled into a rough emotional sea to be overwhelmed and drowned, left only with wide eyes and the daze of fear and no ability to act at all.

Some say that one of the main objects of being alive is to find the balancing point in between these two states of mind; learning how to slide left or right as a situation demands, but to never slip too far, never to lose one's self in either the calm or the storm. Heath's sister might have had something to say about this; Soracia understood how to balance her mind in such a way. It was why she was unstoppable and ruthless when she chose to be.

And so this is where Heath deftly placed herself. In balance.

From this mental perch, she observed her captors with a patient sort of interest, while the rumbling carriage and the cord biting into her wrists and the winter air freezing outside the windows all spoke to her in an anxious chatter. *"Yes, yes,"* she thought to them, assuring. "I can *hear* you. But shush now! I must hear other things as well. . ." The craze of flurries outside had stopped but snowflakes still sat half ready to melt on the fabric of her vest and the end of her nose was pink with cold. —And the High Witch, Locumire sat across from her, menacing, her black and vile emotions filling the rattling cabin. Heath winced and floated back from that, allowing the calm within her to expand, making her head drifty and clear, while the back of her skull tingled steadily. It had been like this before, when she had faced Jenny's mother. But this was different. It was more controlled. More. . .

She looked to her left and to her right, at the two other witches, both older than herself, but clearly younger than Locumire. They sat bristling on either side of her upon the cushioned seat. One had rich brown curls, and the other a shock of black. Both had very pretty faces. (The beautiful are always sought by ones like Locumire.) One also had a cut on her face, which she pressed her fingers to absently, wiping the blood away from where it trickled, all the while being careful not to lower her watch from Heath. Her hand shook slightly, from the excitement and from her youth, and from the heat of dark power which throbbed within her even as it quietly consumed.

She couldn't have been more than twenty years old or so, and yet here she was in a rattling carriage, destroying people's homes, fighting and kidnaping. Murder probably too, if she was a witch of any stature, and whatever other disgraces Locumire could dream up with which to shackle a young woman's soul. —From all Kim had described of her own experiences within the witches' lair, Heath understood more than she would have liked. A place where bravado and outward strength and a numbing of the trembling parts of one's heart were necessary tactics to survive in that world. As Heath gazed at the girl, with her cut cheek and shaking hands, she wondered where the girl's parents were; if they knew their beautiful daughter was so alone. —Who, showing an inkling of magic, had been seduced away from them into such a racing nightmare, with promises and lies and pretty things, —and then with threats and obscenities once she had been safely brought and locked into the bowls of the mountain where dark practices could grow unfettered.

The girl, feeling Heath's gaze penetrating, shifted uncomfortably, "Why are you looking at me like that? Stop it! Do you want me to cut your eyes out?!" She demanded, flexing her bravado with some skill. But Heath could see. Heath could feel beneath all such surfaces when her mind drifted as it did.

"You don't have to be here, you know," she told the girl on an impulse, speaking directly through all of the bravado and armor, right into the center of the girl's trembling soul. "I'll help if you ever need. All you have to do is ask."

F or an instant which surprised them all, a tremulous, living piece within the girl's core rushed up very suddenly and reached like a starved animal. The girl's lips parted, and for half a breath, Heath could see that the girl was only an instant away from bursting into tears, from casting herself desperately to clutch after the life-line Heath had so simply offered...

But only for an instant.

The young woman recoiled, flashing with embarrassment and rage at having been so unexpectedly exposed. Heath gasped as the connection between them, only barely formed, was harshly severed. The girl bolted down her own heart in a fury, making it iron, burying it beneath *iron,* crushing it so that it might never betray her again! She had fought so hard against those very parts of herself which could make her weak with tears and fear that she had learned to *hate* them; to hate her own soul to its very center! *"I'll kill you!"* she hissed, half tears standing on her lashes. "Oh, *I'll kill you* if you ever speak to me like that again!" She turned to her mistress, quaking, seeking approval. *"I'll kill her!"*

Heath regarded the girl with a deep sigh and sank back into her seat. She wondered briefly if there was any hope for such a person, though observing Locumire, she could half understand the mistake. —Platinum hair shining brilliantly in the lamp light, the witch queen appeared powerful and sharp and certain, her eyes like knives, as if she knew exactly what to do and exactly why she was doing it. People are drawn to such things. People will shackle their own souls for such things.

Evil was deceptive, thought Heath. It took for itself and held everything in a jealous clutch for a while, but in the end it was self-destroying. It was obvious. It was sitting right in front of her.

She gazed at Locumire, watching the woman's face relax, smug in expression. "She thinks she is flawless!" Heath realized. "She thinks she is *winning!* But she's only killing these girls, the same way she's killing herself. She doesn't see it! If you lock up your soul like that, feeding not on knowledge or on truths, which yes, can hurt and often do, truth being what it is, —but instead only on sweet lies to yourself, then there is no nourishment! If you feed on only falsehoods and on hate, you will waste away as surely as if you feed on *poison!"*

Heath felt these ideas flowing into her mind as though from somewhere else. . .

t this thought, she gasped, realizing. It was a screed! —Reading itself to her in her own words which drifted up from ages past. She had dwelt long upon this subject before. It was something Trisha had written about in her book, and which Heath had read and which she only now properly understood.

Within her, these pillars of knowledge stood tall and solid, like great tree trunks. But with them came also the bitter understanding that her life here and now might still very well end in failure at the hands of these mixed up, haughty girls and their dark leader.

She ground her teeth as she considered this, dipping somewhat deeply into that storm of frustrated, teary emotion which lapped and swirled hungrily at the edges of her mind. This was all needless! It was stupid. It was futile. And yes, it hurt, because it was not fair.

Locumire leaned forward, catching a wisp of Heath's thinking. "You see, child? All of your ideals are worth nothing here. They are pretty illusions. Only control wrested away from the weak can make the world into what you want it to be. Pretty ideals are as light as tinsel, but outside, the world is unfair and it doesn't care. The only way to win is to recognize this. To put away your silly illusions and know that you must fight until you clutch the very heart of the world in your hand!"

Heath turned her gaze slowly towards the old witch. "It's only that way because of people like you," she said, and then after a thought, added, "And only *to* people like you, by the way. The people I keep near me don't work like that. And they seem to be strong enough to scare you plenty!"

Locumire laughed silkily. "And yet you are here, and they are scattered to the four winds. They are dead by now, I expect."

Heath's heart bucked as that thought penetrated, but she caught herself, recognizing all at once that nothing would please Locumire more than to see her cry, that this was in fact part of the battle. Heath stepped nimbly so that her calm didn't fall and break. She loved her friends, but she could not serve them by losing her composure. Rubel and Varkias wouldn't die so easily, she told herself. And Kim would know enough to bang on a door and ask for help from one of the many neighbors and friends they had made in the market district. Yes. Heath's friends were strong and smart, and Locumire did indeed fear them. As these certainties grew, the lapping waters of pained emotion receded.

"You won't last," Heath said. "You're too daft. And I don't have to lie to myself to like who *I* am. That's the real reason you hate me. That's why I frighten you so much." The two younger witches gaped and then quickly looked at their mistress to see how she would respond. Heath laughed. "I can *see* that, you know. I can see into you, and you are a mess! You are being killed by your own anger and by your own lies to yourself. They feed one another! In fact, you'd be dead right now from it all if some bigger magic wasn't sustaining you; holding you together. —Except with that magic, you are nothing but a slave. Without it you would be nothing. Just a bad joke. I am not the one with illusions!"

Locumire's face went hard for a fraction of a moment, and then she oozed her silky laugh again. "Oh you can see all of that, can you now? Well, perhaps you should let me tell you what *I* can see." She leaned closer, her knife eyes glinting. *"I* can see a little girl who is trying hard to be strong but who really might start to cry at any moment because the little hole in the wall she made with her friends and pretended was a *real* home, has been ruined like the refuse it was! —Garbage found in the alleys and scraped into things you pretended were new. Hum! You are a just little girl in a world of trash all by herself because there was never anyone to call 'Mother' who bothered to love you enough to keep from letting you go; to give you good and proper things which didn't start as the garbage others threw away." Locumire spoke without blinking so that Heath could not look away, but stared back, her eyes round.

"It does not matter how many pretend homes you build," the witch continued, "or how you sometimes wish in secret that silly Kimithin was really your older sister come to take care of you where Soracia is too murderous insane to even *think* about caring. Idiot Kim! As though she really were family. So, Yes, I say you are living in illusions, girl! What else would you call it?"

Heath could say nothing, confused now, feeling her heart prancing in her chest. Locumire leaned still closer and smiled gently, knowing what parts of Heath's soul to press.

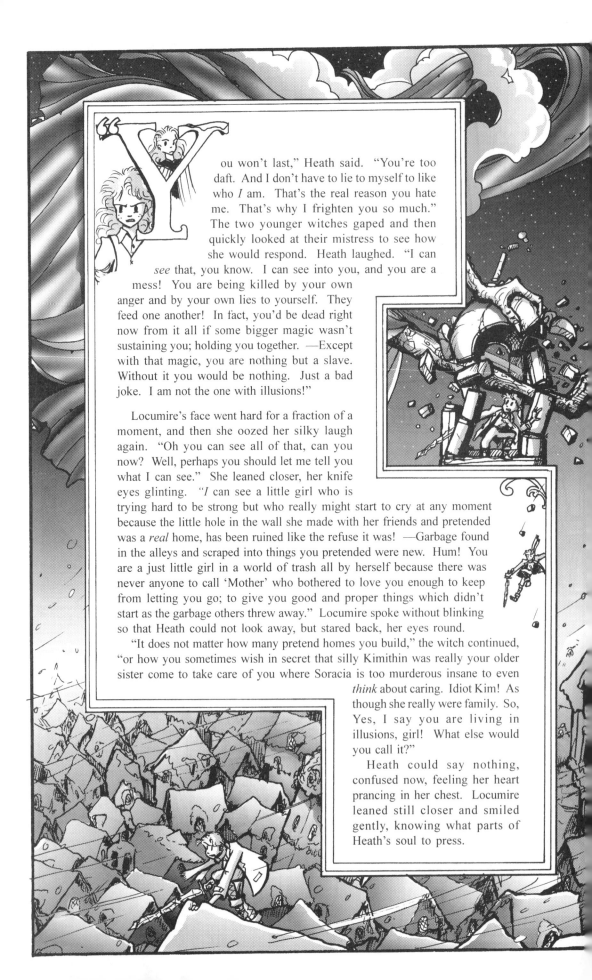

But when it comes right down to it," the witch continued, "Kim has *real* parents. I've met them. They live out in the country side in a lovely little town, and they are worried about their little girl. And one day, when Kim has had enough squalor, she will run back to them and she'll forget all about you and the little hole in the wall you have so selfishly kept her in. She has a *real* family. You don't. Not even the boy. He is *made* of magic. You think you can understand a thief? You think because you have learned a little spell here and there that you can keep him to yourself? My dear. . . You think that one day he will fall to his knee and confess his love to you?" Locumire tilted her head back and laughed sweetly into the air. "Oh, foolish youth!" Her eyes shone as her laughter tinkled, and the two other witches sniggered. "Silly child," she continued, "I will tell you what will *really* happen!

"—You already know it yourself. You can feel it in your heart! You know that one day, Rubel will walk into the forest and he will never come back out again. Simple as that. Already part of him remains there, and every day it is a little more. You have watched him return at night, and you have wished that he would stay, but like Kim, he doesn't belong with you. His home is in the woods, and one day his heart will be there entirely and he will forget all about you. That is how magic boys are. They forget even the ones who love them the best."

"No. . !" the word escaped Heath before she could catch herself. Locumire glowed.

"Oh yes, child. These things are true, and where does that leave you?"

"No, that's wrong!" Heath protested, fighting to tell herself that these things were merely part-truths, crafted by Locumire just to hurt her. —Except they were so very close to how she really felt that it was hard to keep things straight. Locumire was strong tonight, and Heath had been shaken.

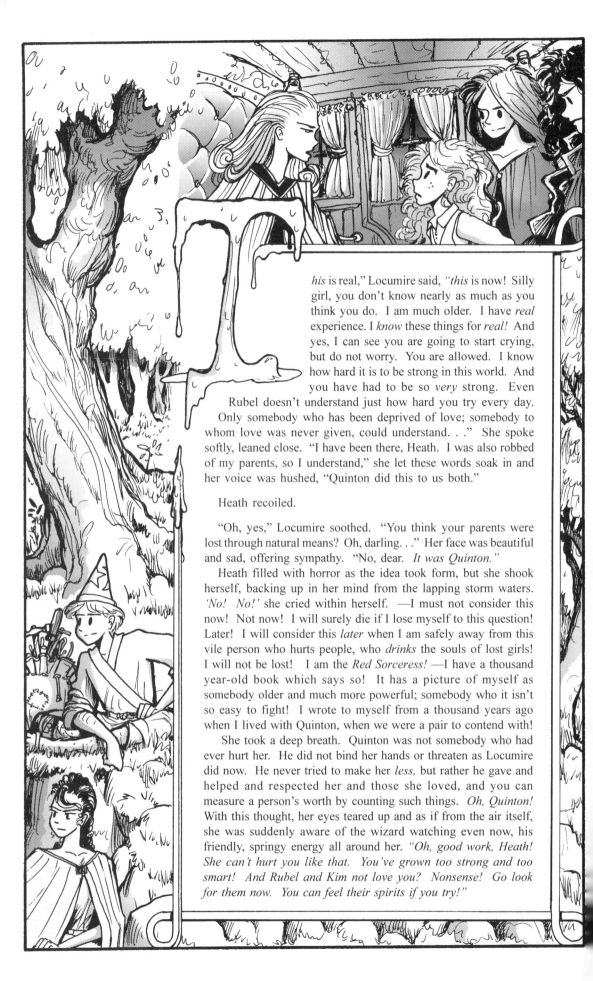

"*his* is real," Locumire said, "*this* is now! Silly girl, you don't know nearly as much as you think you do. I am much older. I have *real* experience. I *know* these things for *real!* And yes, I can see you are going to start crying, but do not worry. You are allowed. I know how hard it is to be strong in this world. And you have had to be so *very* strong. Even Rubel doesn't understand just how hard you try every day. Only somebody who has been deprived of love; somebody to whom love was never given, could understand. . ." She spoke softly, leaned close. "I have been there, Heath. I was also robbed of my parents, so I understand," she let these words soak in and her voice was hushed, "Quinton did this to us both."

Heath recoiled.

"Oh, yes," Locumire soothed. "You think your parents were lost through natural means? Oh, darling. . ." Her face was beautiful and sad, offering sympathy. "No, dear. *It was Quinton.*"

Heath filled with horror as the idea took form, but she shook herself, backing up in her mind from the lapping storm waters. *'No! No!'* she cried within herself. —I must not consider this now! Not now! I will surely die if I lose myself to this question! Later! I will consider this *later* when I am safely away from this vile person who hurts people, who *drinks* the souls of lost girls! I will not be lost! I am the *Red Sorceress!* —I have a thousand year-old book which says so! It has a picture of myself as somebody older and much more powerful; somebody who it isn't so easy to fight! I wrote to myself from a thousand years ago when I lived with Quinton, when we were a pair to contend with!

She took a deep breath. Quinton was not somebody who had ever hurt her. He did not bind her hands or threaten as Locumire did now. He never tried to make her *less,* but rather he gave and helped and respected her and those she loved, and you can measure a person's worth by counting such things. *Oh, Quinton!* With this thought, her eyes teared up and as if from the air itself, she was suddenly aware of the wizard watching even now, his friendly, springy energy all around her. *"Oh, good work, Heath! She can't hurt you like that. You've grown too strong and too smart! And Rubel and Kim not love you? Nonsense! Go look for them now. You can feel their spirits if you try!"*

And she did! Sensing outward like this, she found herself aware of Rubel's warmth and energy. And. . , yes, his *love.* —She could sense Varkias and Kim; neither of whom were dead. Indeed both of them were wondering about her at that very moment. All of them were near, and each had the most unique and wonderful essence. Even Soracia. . . It struck her all at once, being open now to these strange and beautiful winds. She could feel her sister as well. . , and she knew in that moment that Soracia really wasn't evil.

Her sister's soul was strong and hearty and though she did have cynicism and jadedness in measure, Soracia also had the capacity for *more,* just as Rubel had insisted all along.

And so she knew, right then that her family was vital and real! She took a deep breath and the tears balancing on her lashes slid warm down her cheeks. Love tears. She laughed and Locumire squinted at the incongruity, confused as to whether she was winning or losing the fight. Her question was answered abruptly when Heath looked up and shone at her like a sun. Heath could feel her temples and the back of her head exploding with buzzy heat as though she were trying to glow with more energy than she could properly contain. The two witches at her sides crept back unconsciously a space. Heath laughed again and more tears fell.

Locumire was infuriated.

Meeting Heath's gaze, the old witch recognized a thing she did not like at all; that she was sitting before somebody who she could not penetrate or understand, and worst of all, that she was being laughed at. This of all things was unbearable!

Lady Locumire. . , you've had since the summer?" Heath managed to speak, "and *that's* the best you were able to come up with?" She laughed and all the muscles in her stomach bubbled and tickled. Locumire's expression went black. She bared her teeth as she struck. —Hard enough so that Heath's vision was lost in a daze of stars.

"You arrogant little. . !" she sputtered, her rage flooding the cabin. "You will never speak to me in that tone! *Never!*" She struck again. "If you do I'll tear out your tongue. *I'll tear out your eyes!*"

"My eyes?" Heath asked, fire and mirth spilling through her words. "I thought you weren't scared of what I can see. . !"

Locumire emitted a strangled roar and struck her again, harder than before. When the stars eased from Heath's vision, a new fire filled her, blood now running from her nose. She spoke calmly and they all listened in spite of themselves. "If you hit me again," she told them, "I *will* kill you." Locumire couldn't help but hesitate at the tone in the girl's voice. Heath laughed. "Exactly. You *shouldn't* feel sure of yourself. These magic ropes of yours can barely hold me even now, and they're your *best* magic, I can tell! In fact. . ," she paused, testing the energy in the cabin. . . "It's taking all three of you just to hold me here as it is! When your guard slips, and it will very soon, I will be like a fire storm; I shall be able to blast you into a thousand pieces each! And maybe I will. Maybe I will!"

Locumire stiffened in fury, but did not hit her again. Heath exhaled a slow, hot breath, and settled into her seat.

"Behave, girl!" The younger witch barked, holding a knife glowing darkly. "We're only letting you live because you are useful that way. But you can also useful to us dead! If you are not a fool, you will. . ."

Heath shot a look at the girl, whose words and false bravado trailed off into the air. The girl flicked her eyes away rather than touch her line of sight again to Heath's smoldering gaze. —And so the burn of emotions and calm settled once more to the opposite corners of Heath's mind, leaving her to drift small circles through the space in between. . , as though the currents, the very *tides* of the world moved her.

For they did.

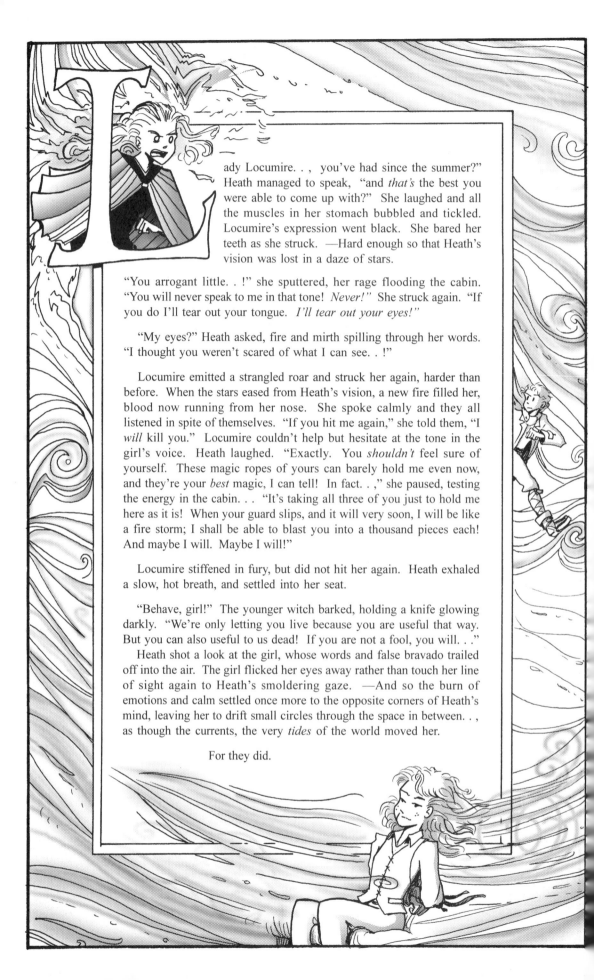

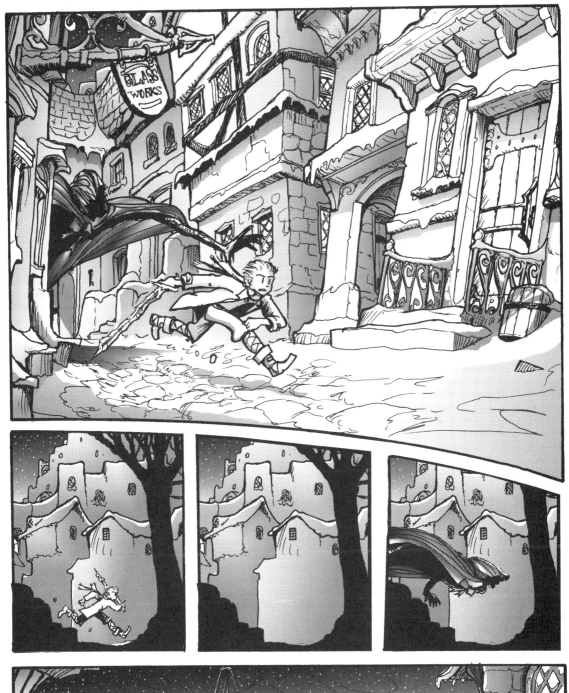

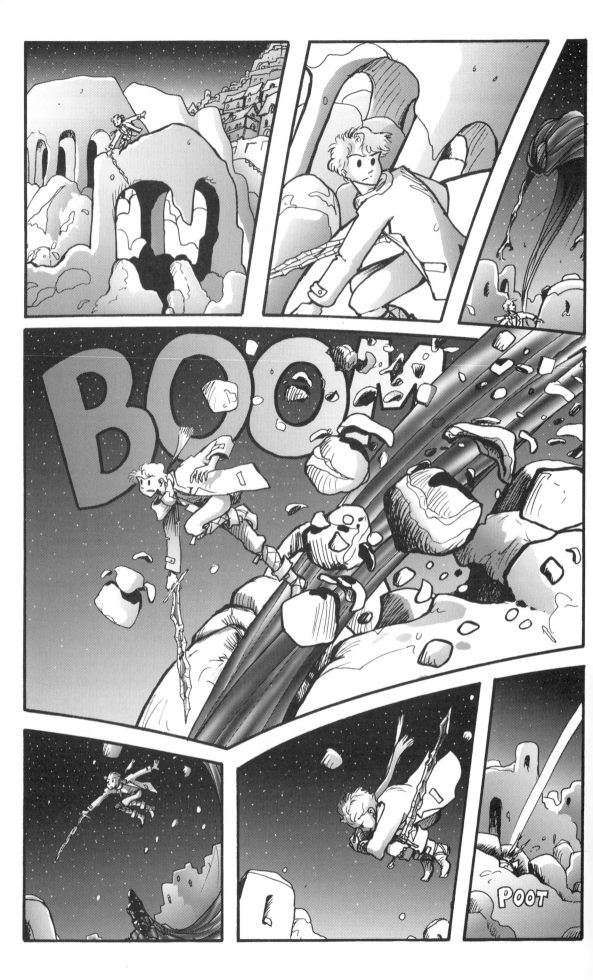

Chapter 6

Chapter 7

—JUST BACK THIS WAY...

EMILIA!

WHERE IS MY SON, EMILIA?

OUT HERE, MA'AM!

WE'RE PLAYING IN THE BACKYARD!

And so Heath listened to the little boy, Varkias guarded the prisoner with half his attention and listened in with his other half, and Kim, her kind heart singing with indignant fury, made a whirlwind of keeping the preening Mrs. Kembridge well occupied. —Each well suited to their tasks.

Dwain cupped his tea tightly and his story whistled like anxious steam from a plugged kettle, his little body shivering, re-living fear. But the drink had been brewed especially to help frightened boys feel brave and Heath was warm and wonderful to talk with. It wasn't long before his peculiar burden began to grow light. Heath nodded and laughed and listened gravely, and soon everybody was feeling much better.

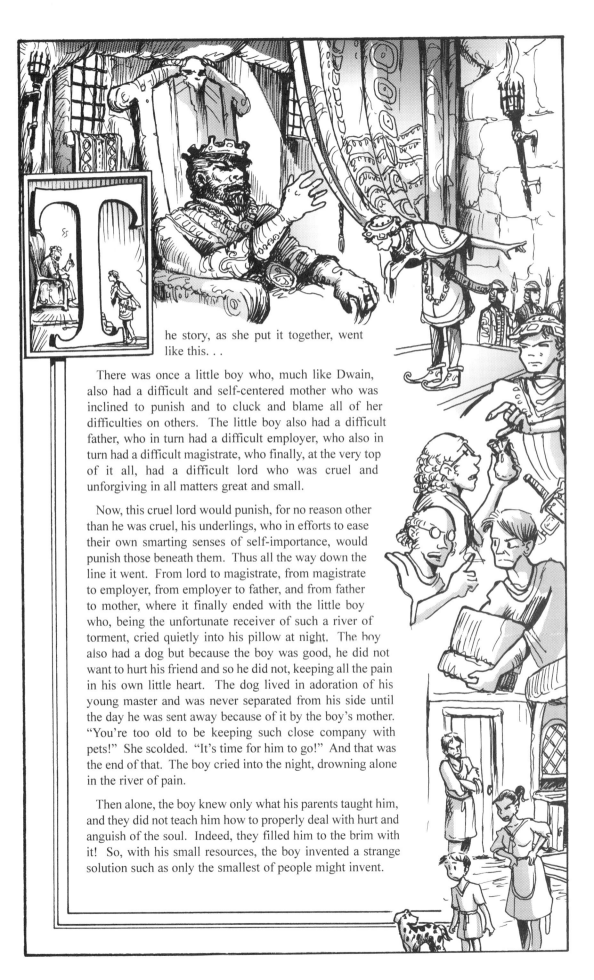

T he story, as she put it together, went like this. . .

There was once a little boy who, much like Dwain, also had a difficult and self-centered mother who was inclined to punish and to cluck and blame all of her difficulties on others. The little boy also had a difficult father, who in turn had a difficult employer, who also in turn had a difficult magistrate, who finally, at the very top of it all, had a difficult lord who was cruel and unforgiving in all matters great and small.

Now, this cruel lord would punish, for no reason other than he was cruel, his underlings, who in efforts to ease their own smarting senses of self-importance, would punish those beneath them. Thus all the way down the line it went. From lord to magistrate, from magistrate to employer, from employer to father, and from father to mother, where it finally ended with the little boy who, being the unfortunate receiver of such a river of torment, cried quietly into his pillow at night. The boy also had a dog but because the boy was good, he did not want to hurt his friend and so he did not, keeping all the pain in his own little heart. The dog lived in adoration of his young master and was never separated from his side until the day he was sent away because of it by the boy's mother. "You're too old to be keeping such close company with pets!" She scolded. "It's time for him to go!" And that was the end of that. The boy cried into the night, drowning alone in the river of pain.

Then alone, the boy knew only what his parents taught him, and they did not teach him how to properly deal with hurt and anguish of the soul. Indeed, they filled him to the brim with it! So, with his small resources, the boy invented a strange solution such as only the smallest of people might invent.

With the edge of a silver coin the boy scratched a rough stick figure of a man on the wall beside his bed and at night he would tell all of his woes to the little picture. And the little picture, being nothing more than a scratching on a wall, could do nothing other than listen. And so it did. And it did. . .

Indeed, the little man listened so well that the boy always felt much better and fell asleep each night in peace.

Now in another place and time, this might have been the end of the matter. But in the city of Highborn of Oceansend where magic lurked and crept, flowing as it did in all the secret ways, the matter did not end there. Thus it was that a roughly drawn little man, the final resting place and focus of so much anxiety. ., began to burn and hurt without knowing why. More and more every night until the very wallpaper upon which he had been created turned yellow and brown, and finally to black as though with soot.

Finally, one evening, years after the boy had grown into a young man and had gone out into the world to find his fortune, the little picture also decided that it no longer wanted to stay. And so, filled with hurt, it picked itself up off the wall and left just like that.

In torment the scribble moved through the world, keeping to walls and wallpaper, seeking endlessly. Seeking without understanding but driven forward nonetheless, like a mosquito only born to the world in the morning it somehow knew by evening what it had been created to do. It soon made a practice of slipping into bed chambers and whispering concentrated pain into unsuspecting ears of sleepers. Several people died in the nights which followed, their hearts naturally open wide in sleep, were overwhelmed and crushed beneath the weight of so much hurt.

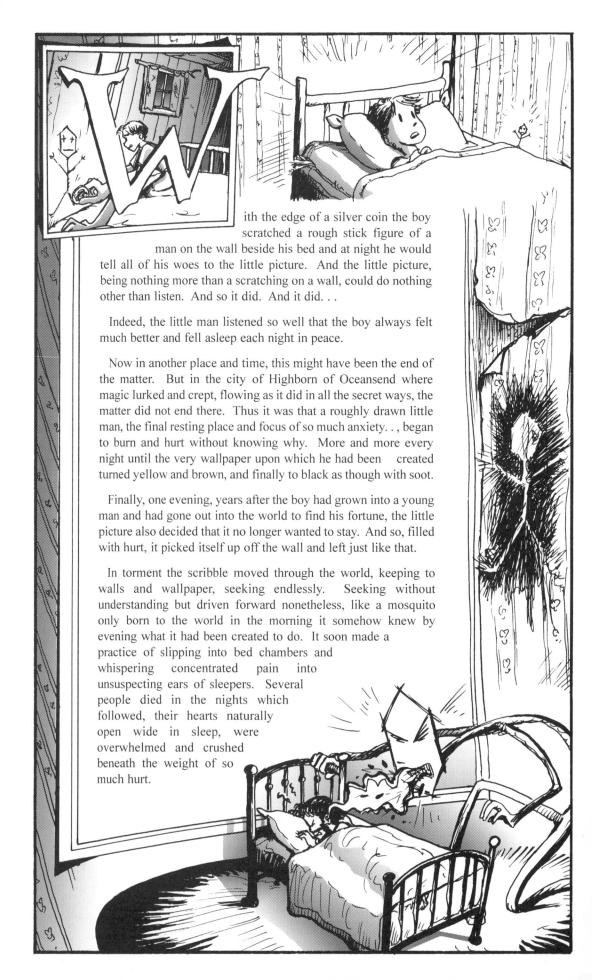

After several night deaths, the community realized that something was amis and a local mage was consulted. —He was not especially powerful or famous, but he was earnest in his work and the only wizard to be found in a time of crisis and so the people were eager for his help. Thus, after many trials and troubles, the mystery was solved and the scribble was trapped.

The family whose home it had been discovered in was convinced to quickly abandon their property. In a single day, they moved so that before nightfall, the doorway could be bricked up tight. The mage laid what spells he could muster to keep the chamber sealed, and that was that. The scribble wailed and scuttled about inside its makeshift prison, but in vain. It was trapped. And so the community let out a long sigh of relief, and diligently set about the task of forgetting all about it.

Heath, however, was not the sort who liked to forget things, and so she pondered and wondered about what she ought to do. . .

She wasn't about to keep it inside her backpack for another hundred years. It was her favorite backpack, after all.

"Couldn't we just tear the paper in half?" Rubel offered while discussing the problem later that evening. "Or maybe if I fought it with the glass sword. --I left it with Soracia, but I could go and-"

"No." Heath shook her head. "This isn't a normal kind of situation. I don't think the scribble is bad on purpose. It wouldn't be fair to just kill it. I want to try to undo what made it. Give it a chance."

"Hm." Rubel frowned. "You always pick the most difficult way."

"I hope you can figure out how to solve this," Kim put in. "And then you could show me. Hate and mean energy is what I was surrounded by the whole time before I left Locumire's palace. I'd sure like to know how to undo stuff like that!"

"Is it even possible?" Rubel asked.

"It might be," Heath said. "The scribble didn't choose. And it doesn't know how to deal with what it is. If I can show it how, then maybe that will be enough and it will be able to unravel all on its own. —It's quite an ugly knot of dark energy. I was looking at it earlier."

"But if you can't?"

"Hm." Heath was silent for a long time before looking up. "Then you can kill it."

Rubel nodded. "Okay. But be careful, alright? Don't do something dumb like take all of its bad energy into you. That wouldn't be good, Heath. That would be awful!"

"I won't."

Rubel measured her, frowning. "I know what you're like. You better promise me."

Heath grinned up at him. "Okay, fine. I *promise.*"

Rubel nodded again, satisfied, and Heath wanted all at once to hug him, but instead she didn't.

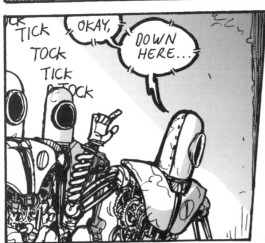

Chapter 8

There once was a girl who lived in a grand palace far up on a mountain top which overlooked a grand city. In this palace, the girl slept and ate and went about her daily chores, which consisted in part of strutting and fuming and grinding her teeth so that all the other girls would watch her in awe and stand aside when she stomped by. —Her day also consisted of chasing about after a tall and beautiful witch queen with white hair and a sharp eye. The witch queen swept from blowing balconys to cold dungeons, executing all the dark and dramatic duties which fell to witch queens.

The girl was also an apt student, for she had an angry streak within which often showed itself. The witch queen observed quietly, and spoke to this part of the girl, encouraging it into greater strength and deeper bitterness with each passing day. But still, the cruelness was not yet solidified, for the girl was still young, and young girls are changeable creatures, casting about, searching for who they will grow up to be. Indeed, there were some days when all alone, the girl would sit by herself and quietly weep for her mother and her lost friends and for the country home where she had been a child.

On private days such as these, she would wonder if she was truly in the right place at all, high above the city in so grand a palace.

And so it went.

Now, one day, Leahanna, for that was her name, chanced to fall in love. —Which was a foolish thing to do, for the boy she fell in love with was none other than the prince.

The prince had long ago finished being a changeable creature; he had grown up and had sold his heart in exchange for power, thus he no longer had a heart to give to any girl. Leahanna, being a smart and apt student, recognized this at once, but love is an unexpected thing which rarely makes allowances for youth! And so her heart broke on a daily basis, and her mistress tilted her head and laughed.

"Silly girl!" The witch queen cooed. "Did I not tell you that your heart would break? He laughs at you and he uses you. —You who, through all I have given you, could become the most powerful one of all! But instead you allow yourself to be a toy in his hands. He will never love you. You are a fool, and one day you will see. One day soon, perhaps your love will turn to rage, and then you will be free. I will show you *how* if you like..."

Leahanna said nothing and bowed her head in shame, for she knew that she was a fool, but her heart was still seeped with hurt and love, and so she went through her days, hoping, hoping.

"I wish Kim were here," she thought. "She wouldn't laugh at me. Now that she is gone, I love her more than ever. But I cannot ever see her again. If I do, she will only see that she was right all along, and that I was wrong, and I will not give her that! Damn her, anyway! It isn't fair."

SIGH WHAT ELSE IS NEW?

WELL, I GUESS I DON'T NEED TO GO OUT FOR BREAD AND EGGS NOW... OR CHEESE... DINNER IS PRACTICALLY MADE RIGHT HERE!

YEAH. THIS HEALING THING IS SURE TURNING OUT TO BE GOOD THAT WAY. YOU WANNA HELP ME UPSTAIRS? I COULD USE ANOTHER SET OF HANDS. WHAT FOR?

MRS. KOVICKS IS COMING IN A SHORT WHILE ABOUT HER HIP, AND I STILL NEED THOSE SILKWEEDS WRAPPED AND DRYING BEFORE TONIGHT. YOU DON'T REALLY NEED ME.

YOU WERE GOING TO GET MRS. KOVICKS TO HELP YOU WRAP THEM UP. THAT'S HOW YOU WORK BEST. YOU DISTRACT PEOPLE FOR A WHILE SO THEY DON'T WORRY SO MUCH ABOUT THEIR PROBLEMS.

WELL.., IT'S ONE WAY... I JUST NEED TO GET OUT FOR A WALK ON MY OWN FOR A WHILE. OR SOMETHING...

OKAY... I'LL SEE YOU LATER..? YEAH. SURE.

"YOU HAD BETTER HOPE SO."

"DESPITE HER VANITY AND HER MANY WEAKNESSES... LOCUMIRE IS STILL A VILLAIN WITH MUCH PATIENCE AND CRAFT."

"MUCH HATE."
"HER AIM WAS TO BIND YOU TO RUBEL."
"TO MAKE THE BLAZING HEART OF THE RED SORCERESS GROW COLD AND BREAK."

"—WITH A BROKEN HEART, HEATH CAN BE DEFEATED."
"HEATH'S HEART WILL BREAK..?"

"WHAT DID YOU THINK? — YOU HAVE SEEN IT AS WELL AS I."
"IT WILL ONLY GROW STRONGER WITH EACH PASSING DAY..."
"HEATH IS GROWING QUICKLY."
"SHE WILL BE A YOUNG WOMAN SOON..."
"A FEW MORE SPRINGTIMES AND IT WILL BE OVER FOR YOU."

"YOU THINK SHE IS BRIGHT NOW? HA! I HAVE SEEN THIS BEFORE, AND I CAN PROMISE THAT YOU WILL BE NOTHING BUT A SPECK OF SHADOW IN HER SUN!"
"HER POWER WILL FLOW OVER THIS CITY LIKE A TIDE OF GOLDEN LIGHT, AND RUBEL WILL LOVE HER AND LIVE FOR HER ALONE..."

Chapter 9

Soracia, blinding quick, slipped from the water and was airborne in a thrice, avoiding the magical blade by a hair's breadth. Jale followed, little more than a blur. She meant to kill! —Words and meekness and long suffering patience now finally abandoned, old instincts raced through the child like a forest fire. With a ferocious snarl, she spread her arms and was consumed! Rage has always been a last answer to confusion; obliterating uncertainty in the furnace of mad emotion.

Soracia did not even bother trying to speak to the girl. She understood rage. Instead she flew as fast as she was able, twisting the space around her so that the thirsting black razor could not find its way. It was difficult; she and the sword had fought hilt in hand together a thousand times; there was no possibility of secrecy lying between them. The Lady Soracia, whose power rested in half through the knowing and keeping of secrets, was not entirely certain what the outcome of this contest would be.

Her skin recoiled as from a too hot sun when the magical blade sizzled through the air an eyelash from her cheek. Soracia dodged and spun and flew, perilously close to injury, her mind racing and scolding inwardly. Tight, she slipped between a murderous attack which would have left any other warrior in three pieces. Not tight enough. With a twin crack, the two magic swords she had summoned as replacements were each cut clean through. Their magic, a shimmer of silver smoke, lost itself in the air. Kim squinted bitter-eyed at the victory and leaped again.

he battle went on for some time more, crossing back and forth the water and the beach, the two sorceresses eerily similar in their movements and expressions. Kim in fury and fire, and Soracia's strained patience flashing between expressions of annoyance and regret. There were no onlookers upon the shore, —the greatest of conflicts often happening in private. But had anybody been present to witness might well have thought that it was a mother and her daughter who fought across the sand that day.

In the end, Soracia's frustration outgrew her other conflicted feelings. There was an opening and she took it, her leg sliding through the air, a soft flicker, tapping Kim in the eye with the knot of bone at her ankle so that the girl sputtered in pain. Kim saw stars and lost her place in the fight.

She was not used to being struck.

Soracia pressed the advantage. With a gust of power summoned from her belly, a sheet of salt water and sand exploded up just in time for Jale to inhale. It burst into her lungs, grainy and sharp and Kim, now blinded, choked and flung herself wildly. The black sword screamed through the air, but the outcome of the fight was no longer in question.

Soracia struck again, not hard, catching the girl in her stomach. Kim crumpled at once, gasping. The black blade winked out of existence and Kim was small and meek and defeated once more. The girl knelt on the warm sand, sobbing.

Settling to the beach, the sand accepting Soracia's feet in its supple dryness. Somewhere in the battle, her boots had vanished, exploded to tatters; she was still not used to wearing mortal clothes.

"Jale," she said, relaxing, owning the victory as though it had been assured from the beginning of time. "Oh, my dear. . ."

"Just leave me alone," the girl cried, defeat and shame bright red upon her face. Her tears flowed and dripped and were lost on the sand among the sun bleached chips of drift wood and fragments of sea silk. Her fury too was spent and lost. "Just leave me be," she begged. "Why can't everyone just leave me be?"

"I am sorry, my dear," Soracia said, kneeling at her side, wanting to see Kim's face. The girl turned her head away, her hair falling between them, a thin veil moving in the breeze. A strong feeling of compassion, of shame rose like bile at the back of Soracia's throat. "I am sorry," she repeated. "But you must understand that I cannot allow you to harm her. Heath is my sister. I want you to make the right choice. That's all. I do not want to have to do this again."

Kim said nothing, turning her head further away, her little soul wanting nothing more than to hide, to lose itself within the cool and merciful roar of surf upon the shores of Oceansend.

Epilogue

Last Page of the Story.

Hello and goodbye once again!

Winter has passed and Spring time has come, and with it the beginnings of new adventures and challenges for everybody. At the time of my writing these parting words, I had already begun drawing the first pages of the next book. Kim and Leahanna figure significantly into the story, of course, as long ago I had hoped they would. —Back when I first painted the two sword girls, airbrushing highlights into Kim's long hair. It was on the cover of the 8th issue of the comic book series where *Thieves & Kings* was born, and boy, that was a long time ago! Theirs is a story I wasn't sure I'd ever get around to telling. But, hey, here we are!

I also have several scripts written and waiting for me at the drafting board which deal with the challenges Heath her gang will get to face over their next year together. —And it *is* turning into that. Heath's *gang,* I mean. Rubel provides stability and safety and resources and all of that, but Heath is without question the natural leader of their group. She knows which way the ship is pointing and why it must sail. It's a dynamic I was expecting, but was still really happy to see as it unfolded. Heath is just one of those people around whom the world naturally likes to revolve.

And Soracia... She keeps surprising me, too. I am finding that I like her character more with each passing year. It's a little heart-breaking to see her so awkward and uncertain in her new role, but I have a lot of respect for her in her making the effort to change. In any case, it would be lunacy to underestimate what she is still very much capable of. She has not yet finished shaking the world, and I look forward to spending more time with her in the next couple of books to see how she does it!

As for shaking the world... I wrote some important scripts for Katara two years back, and they are steadily getting closer to the top of my to-draw list. I think she is going to surprise everybody; it sure surprised me anyway, when I finally worked out the full scope of what she has planned. It was exciting to see the meaning behind all the little hints and tells my subconscious writer has been casually dropping ever since I first put pen and pencil to paper ten years ago!

So that's all for now! I very much hope you enjoyed this book, and I wish you well in your lives and all that comes your way!

Cheers to you!

—Mark Oakley